Pillow

Places

Joseph Kuefler

Balzer + Bray
An Imprint of HarperCollins *Publishers*

To Isaac, Wesley, Harrison, Robert, and Alma—
may your world be filled with pillow feathers

Pillows.

Couch pillows.

Bed pillows.

Stack them high
above your head pillows.

What should we make pillows.
What will it be pillows.

Climb aboard and
come with me pillows.

Pillow lava on the sun.

Pillow laughing.
Pillow fun.

Pillows.

Pillow lifting.
Pillow piling.

Pillow building.
Pillow smiling.

Striped pillows.

Spotted, plaid, and white pillows.

Royal battle pillow fight pillows.

Where should we go pillows.
What should we be pillows.
Imagine all the things we'll see pillows.

Pillow friends we
will always keep.

Pillow starlight.

Pillow sleep.

Balzer + Bray
is an imprint of HarperCollins Publishers.

Pillow Places

ISBN 978-0-06-295673-6

Typography by Joseph Kuefler and Dana Fritts
21 22 23 24 25   RTLO   10 9 8 7 6 5 4 3 2 1

❖

First Edition